D0498577

HOCUS POCUS HOTEL

Hocus Pocus Hotel is published by Capstone
1710 Roe Crest Dr .
North Mankato, Minnesota 56003
www.capstoneyoungreaders.com

Summary: Abracadabra reveals himself, but even the greatest magician ever known can't control all of the magic happening at the Abracadabra Hotel.

Cataloging-in-Publication Data is available at the Library of Congress website.

ISBN: 978-1-4342-4721-6 (paper-over-board)

This book is also available in two library-bound editions:
The Assistant Vanishes! 978-1-4342-4101-6
The Trouble with Abracadabra 978-1-4342-4102-3

Designer: Kay Fraser
Photo credits: Shutterstock
Abracadabra Hotel illustration: Brann Garvey

Printed in China
092012
006934LEOS13

The Return of Abracadabra

BOOK 2

by Michael Dahl

illustrated by Lisa K. Weber

capstone

3 THE ABRACADABRA HOTEL

Table of

Contents

1 The Premiere

On Friday at three o'clock, Tyler Yu and Charlie Hitchcock stood together just inside the back doors of Blackstone Middle School.

Each of them clutched a packet of bright yellow paper. All around them, other students

took books from their lockers, packed their bags, and made plans for the weekend.

It was an ordinary Friday afternoon. There was nothing at all unusual about the scene.

Except that Ty was the biggest bully in school, and Charlie was a bookworm best known for his photographic memory, and they weren't supposed to be friends.

"Okay," Ty said, looking down the hall. "This is where we split up."

Charlie nodded.

"I'll hand out flyers to the eighth-graders," Ty went on. "I'll also hand out flyers to the jocks, the cool kids, the cheerleaders, and the crew in detention."

"Who does that leave for me?" Charlie asked, looking up at Ty.

"The dorks," Ty said. He shrugged. "And the nerds."

Charlie rolled his eyes. "Don't forget the geeks."

"Them too," Ty agreed. He pointed toward the science wing. "You go that way."

"Obviously," Charlie said. He walked off into the crowd.

"And remember—you don't know me," Ty called after him.

Charlie reached the first corner and stopped. Then he turned and saw Ty across the main hallway, handing some yellow sheets to two eighth-grade girls.

"I think everyone will figure out that we know each other," Charlie hollered, "when they realize that we're handing out the exact same flyers!"

Smiling, he headed down the science hallway.

He would never have tried something like that a few weeks ago, but ever since Charlie helped Ty solve two magic mysteries at the Abracadabra Hotel, the two boys had become something like friends.

Ty would probably deny that.

Actually, Charlie was sure Ty would deny that.

But he knew it was true.

Thirty minutes later, the boys met up at the front of the school. All the flyers were handed out, except one, which Charlie still held in both hands.

"Why did you save that one?" Ty said. "Did you give one to every kid?"

Charlie nodded.

"Chess club?" Ty asked.

"Yup," said Charlie.

"Computer club?" Ty asked.

"Of course," said Charlie.

"What about the chemistry club?" Ty suggested.

"Got 'em," Charlie said. "I promise. I got everyone. This one is to hang up."

Charlie led the way to the office bulletin board. He handed the flyer to Ty. "Hold this," he said. Then Charlie pulled two tacks from his pocket, took the flyer back from Ty, and tacked it into place on the bulletin board.

"There," Charlie said. The boys stood back and looked at the flyer.

is proud to present

ITS FIRST MAGIC SHOW
IN FIFTY YEARS

TWO SHOWS THIS SATURDAY
12 NOON AND 7 P.M.

FEATURING

MADAME KRZYSCKY, THE FIRE-EATER
MIND-READING HYPNOTISM BY
THE GREAT PROFESSOR PONTIFICATE
THE AMAZING MR. THURSDAY, JUGGLER
AND ALL THE WAY FROM THE LOST KINGDOM OF GILJARRI . . .
EXPLORER OF MAGICAL REALMS . . . MASTER OF DIMENSIONAL POWERS
BEYOND YOUR WILDEST IMAGININGS . . .
THE GREATEST PERFORMER OF OUR AGE OR ANY AGE . . . .

THE GREAT AND POWERFUL
THEOPOLIS!

2
Like New

Everyone at the Abracadabra Hotel had a job to do for the hotel's first magic show in decades.

Ty's job was to collect tickets. Before the show started, he stood at the door to the old theater. He tugged at the tight collar of his maroon tuxedo. There were still a few minutes until showtime.

"That's a good look for you," Charlie said, walking over. He wore a simple dark suit. Everyone attending would be dressed up, like they did in the old days to go to the theater. He sat down on an old, red velvet bench near Ty's door.

Everything in the old theater had been cleaned and refurbished for the big opening night. The bench looked like it had been made yesterday, even though it was almost sixty years old—as old as the hotel itself. Even the old carved Tragedy and Comedy faces on the theater's double doors had been polished within an inch of their lives.

Just then, Brack walked up.

"Hello, young gentlemen," he said.

Brack was the old elevator operator, but he had a secret too, a secret as old as the hotel itself. And Charlie was the first person to discover it.

Brack was actually Mr. Abracadabra, the founder and namesake of the hotel and one of the most famous magicians of all time.

Charlie was the only one who knew.

Brack had organized this magic show. He wanted to bring the spotlight back to the Abracadabra Hotel for one last amazing show, but today's show wasn't the full spectacle he had in mind. It was a kind of dress rehearsal for the really big show.

Charlie couldn't wait. But in the meantime, he couldn't tell anyone that he knew Brack was anyone other than the elevator operator.

Today, Brack wasn't wearing his old-fashioned elevator operator uniform. Instead, he was dressed to the nines in a tuxedo with tails, a top hat, and a cane.

Ty shook his head slowly. "That is totally not fair," he grumbled quietly to Charlie. "Brack wears that cool tux, and I'm stuck dressed like a couch."

Charlie chuckled. "Is it just about showtime?" he asked.

The old man pulled a gold watch from his pocket. It swung at the end of a long, thin gold chain.

"Nice watch," Ty said.

"Thank you," Brack said, admiring the antique. "It's older than this hotel. It's older than I am. In fact, I don't know how old it is."

Charlie tried to get a glimpse of the watch as Brack twirled it on its chain.

"Would you like to see it?" Brack asked. He stopped it from swinging, caught it in his palm with a thump, and held it out to the boys.

"Thanks," Charlie said, grinning. He grabbed the watch. The chain was quite long. He held it between himself and Ty so they could both get a look at it. The watch had exposed gears—it looked like dozens of them. It ticked and tocked loudly. When Ty hit a little button on top, the face swung open so they could see the time.

Two minutes to noon. The show was about to start.

"Thanks, Brack," Charlie said. He handed the watch back and added, "You better get to your seat."

"And you boys better get inside too," he said, walking past them. "I don't think you'll want to miss this show."

The boys watched Brack walk down the long aisle toward his special box in the front.

"He's up to something," Ty said.

Charlie shrugged. "Of course he is," he said. "He always is."

3
The Great and Powerful Theopolis

Charlie and Ty headed into the darkening theater. Their seats were in the very front row of the balcony. They were far away from the stage, but they could see almost the whole theater.

The spotlight thumped on, pointing right at

Brack in his special box. He stood up and waved. The crowd clapped.

"Ladies and gentlemen," Brack said, "and children of all ages! Welcome to the first performance of magic, illusion, and intrigue at Abracadabra Hotel in fifty years."

The crowd clapped and cheered. Charlie spotted a whole bunch of kids he recognized from school. They were all sitting in a group in the section behind Brack. The rest of the theater was sparsely filled, mostly with guests from the hotel.

"Enjoy the show," Brack said, and the spotlight switched off.

The curtain went up, and the stage was lit. Charlie took a deep breath.

The fire-eater was very exciting. The kids from Blackstone Middle School cheered and hollered when Madame Krzyscky swallowed a flaming sword as her grand finale.

Professor Pontificate, the mind reader and

hypnotist, convinced one of the hotel guests that she was a chicken. For the rest of the show, the poor woman waddled around the theater saying, "Cluck, cluck!" and trying to eat worms from the floor.

Mr. Thursday had spent hours practicing, and it showed. His juggling act was wonderful. But everyone was waiting for the main attraction. At last, it was time for the Great Theopolis of Giljarri!

The stage filled with smoke. A heavy black curtain closed across the middle of the stage, adding an air of gravity. Thunder clapped in the catwalks. Laughter—deep and dark and scary—filled the auditorium.

Then a baritone voice boomed over the PA system: "Beware! We the demons of the Kingdom of Giljarri unleash the Great and Powerful Theopolis!"

There was one more flash of lightning, and one more great clap of thunder, and there, in the middle of the stage, appeared the Great and Powerful Theopolis himself. He wore a long, shining black robe, with a hood up over his head. He stuck out his arms and threw his head back. The hood flipped off.

The kids from Blackstone went crazy cheering.

"Wow," Charlie said. "You'd think they were all big fans or something."

Ty was on his feet, clapping like mad. "After an entrance like that, who wouldn't be?" he said, eyes on the stage.

Charlie shrugged. He didn't think it was such a big deal. Anyone could use a smoke machine and similar special effects. He wanted to see some impressive illusions. Then he'd think about becoming a fan.

The first few magic tricks Theopolis performed were nothing special. He sawed his assistant in half, levitated a piano, and produced a demon from the "Kingdom of Giljarri."

Charlie could tell how each trick was done, even from way up in the balcony. He kept whispering the magician's technique to Ty, but finally Ty turned and said, "Quit it. You're ruining the fun."

"Sorry," Charlie muttered. "To me, figuring it out is the fun part."

"For my finale," Theopolis announced, "I will need a volunteer."

Hands shot up all over the theater. Ty jumped to his feet and waved wildly.

"How are you going to volunteer from way up here?" Charlie said.

"Oh yeah," Ty said. He sat down.

"I'm told," Theopolis said, "that there is a large group from the local middle school here today."

"Who told him?" Charlie asked.

Ty shrugged. "Not me," he said.

The kids from Blackstone cheered and hollered. Theopolis smiled at them. "Perhaps

one of you would make a good volunteer," he said. "Perhaps . . . you!"

He pointed at a boy right in the middle of the large group of kids. Charlie recognized the boy, but didn't know his name.

"Lucky kid," Ty said. "Man, I can't wait to talk to him about this at school on Monday."

"You know him?" Charlie said.

Ty nodded. "Yeah," he said. "I gave him the flyer yesterday. His name's Paul Juke. It was funny, actually. He was the only kid I gave a flyer to who already knew about the show."

On the stage, Theopolis and Paul watched as two stagehands—both dressed in hooded robes—wheeled on a huge wardrobe. They placed it in the center of the stage, right up against the heavy black curtain. The wardrobe was made of wood and looked older than the hotel.

Charlie rolled his eyes. "I've seen this wardrobe," he said. "That's the same wardrobe they used in the 1950s. It has a false bottom, and it's over the trapdoor. Brack showed me the other day."

"Quiet!" Ty said. "Don't ruin the trick."

"This wardrobe," Theopolis announced from the stage in his booming, demonic voice, "was used during the last show, fifty years ago. Back then, they put in a volunteer, closed the door,

and said a few magic words. The person inside would disappear."

The crowd oohed and ahhed.

"But today, I'll be doing things a little differently," Theopolis said. "Anyone can open a trapdoor. But for today's performances, I've had the trapdoors in this stage nailed closed."

Charlie leaned forward.

"I will make this boy, this brave volunteer, truly vanish," Theopolis said. "This will be no illusion. It will be genuine magic, magic I learned from the demons of Giljarri."

Paul stepped into the wardrobe. Theopolis closed the door behind him. He locked it with a key, and carefully slipped the key into a pocket in his robe.

He pulled on his hood, and the lights dimmed. Smoke flowed across the stage floor. The demon voices cackled and boomed. Theopolis muttered words in a language no one could understand.

"The boy is ours now," said the deep voices.

Thunder clapped and lightning streaked across the theater.

Suddenly the stage lights came back up. Theopolis pulled off his hood.

"It is done," he said, pulling the key from his pocket. "Behold!"

He opened the wardrobe.

Paul was gone.

The crowd went wild. Theopolis stepped up to the edge of the stage and bowed deeply several times.

When the cheering died down, he put up his arms and announced, "Thank you for coming. Good night." As he spoke, the hooded stagehands returned. They wheeled the wardrobe away.

A confused murmur ran across the theater. "Where is the boy?" voices said. "Isn't he going to bring him back?"

"My friends, my friends," Theopolis said, trying to calm the crowd. Charlie noticed he was smiling. "I will produce the boy at the evening show."

The houselights came up, and Theopolis dashed backstage.

"That was weird," Ty said. "And you have to admit, pretty amazing."

Charlie frowned. "Let's go check it out," he said. "Something's fishy with this guy."

"Of course something's fishy with this guy," Ty said. "He's a demon master!"

Charlie rolled his eyes. "Let's go," he said, tugging on Ty's maroon sleeve.

"Fine," Ty said. "Just make sure no one from school sees us hanging out together."

The boys hurried down to the stage level. As the crowd slowly filed out, Charlie followed Ty onto the stage.

"Hey, who's that over there?" asked Charlie. Some kids were half-hidden in the shadows just offstage.

"They're just some of your nerd friends from

the A/V Club," said Ty. "Annie said they asked to film the show for a school project."

"They're not nerds," Charlie said, frowning. "They're geeks. There's a difference: geeks are smarter."

"Whatever," said Ty. "Your geek friends, then."

Charlie rolled his eyes. Then he quickly found the trapdoor in the stage—the one they used to use for disappearing acts like this one. Rows of shiny nailheads marked the sides.

"Look," Charlie said, squatting near the trapdoor. "He wasn't lying. It really has been nailed shut."

Ty stood next to Charlie and crossed his arms. "There's no mystery here," he said. "The Great Theopolis is a real magician."

Charlie stood and shook his head. "I'll figure it out," he said, looking around, "and I'll start with that wardrobe. Where is it?"

"The stagehands probably would have put

it back in storage, under the stage," Ty said. "Follow me."

In the center of the big, dusty, musty under-stage space, the boys found the wardrobe they were looking for.

Charlie pulled open the doors. It was very big—bigger than he could have guessed from the balcony. The inside was blond wood, but the outside had been painted red with a bright gold trim.

"What are we looking for?" Ty said.

"First of all, Paul," Charlie said.

"He's not inside," Ty said. "Now what?"

Charlie didn't answer. He felt around the box, looking for secret doors or handles or anything. On the floor of the wardrobe, he found a hidden switch. The floor snapped and swung down, but not all the way.

"If this were over the trapdoor in the stage, it would open all the way," Charlie said.

"Right," said Ty. "If the trapdoor wasn't

nailed down. Then the person inside could drop down into this room."

Charlie nodded. "Of course, we already checked the stage trapdoor, and it was sealed," he said. He stared into the open wardrobe. "Something's not right here," he said, tapping his chin.

"Uh, yeah," Ty said. "Paul is missing. It's why we're here, remember?"

"That's not what I mean," Charlie said. "I mean—"

But he didn't finish his thought, because at that very moment, a light flashed in his eyes.

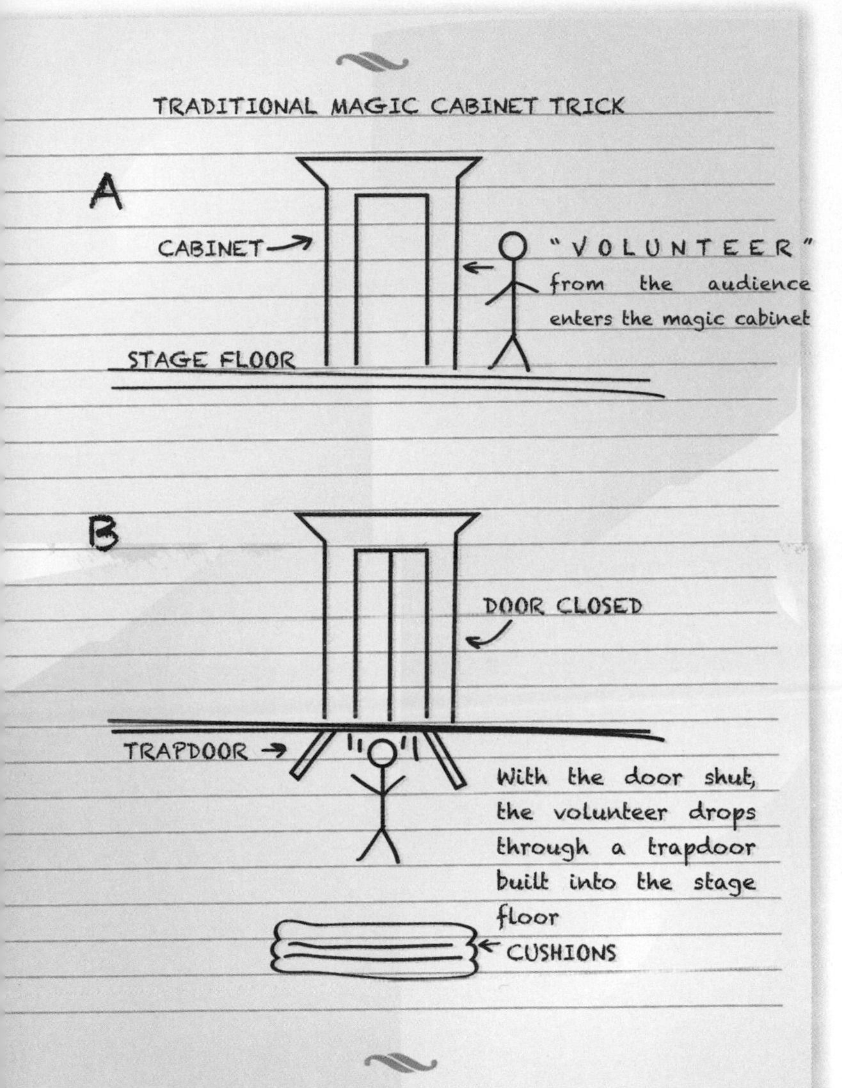
TRADITIONAL MAGIC CABINET TRICK
A
CABINET
"VOLUNTEER"
from the audience
enters the magic cabinet
STAGE FLOOR
B
DOOR CLOSED
TRAPDOOR
With the door shut,
the volunteer drops
through a trapdoor
built into the stage
floor
CUSHIONS

Joey Bingham, Reporter

"Perfect!" said . . . someone. Charlie couldn't see well enough yet to know who.

"Who are you?" Ty asked.

Charlie squinted. Ty rubbed his eyes.

"Oh, sorry about the flash," said a young

man. He held a big, old-fashioned camera. "It's just too dark down here to shoot without it."

"Why are you taking our picture?" Charlie asked.

"Well, I wanted a good shot of the magic wardrobe," the man said. "Having a couple of kids in the picture seemed like good idea, for that human-interest angle. I'm Joey Bingham, by the way. I'm a reporter for Channel Fifty."

"I thought I recognized you," Ty said.

"Recognized him?" Charlie said. "I can still hardly see him." He rubbed at his eyes with his fists.

Bingham let the camera hang from a strap around his neck. Then he picked up another camera that was also hanging from his neck. This time, it was a video camera. He switched it on. "Did either of you know the missing boy?" Bingham asked in a deep newscaster voice.

"Wait, are you filming us?" Ty asked, backing away.

"Of course," Bingham said. He followed Ty with the camera. "Don't you want to be on TV?"

"No!" Ty said, hurrying behind the wardrobe. "Especially not with Hitchcock. It'll ruin my reputation."

"Your name is Hitchcock? You mean like the scary movie director?" said Bingham.

Charlie nodded. He sometimes got tired having to explain his last name to people.

"That could be an angle for my story," said Bingham. "You see, it's just like a Hitchcock film. Some unsuspecting person disappears, and then—"

"Uh, he's a student at Blackstone Middle School," Charlie said as the reporter pointed the camera at him. "The kid who disappeared, I mean. I don't know him, though. Paul something."

"Paul Juke," Ty said, jumping out from behind the wardrobe. "His name's Paul Juke. He's in my technology class."

"Great," Bingham said. "Let's get something

out to the station. They can have an interview on the air in two minutes."

"An interview?" Charlie said. "Just because of a magic trick?"

"Of course!" said Theopolis in his booming voice.

Everyone turned to look as the magician came into the storage room, still wearing his mysterious black robe. "Because this was no simple magic trick."

Bingham excitedly turned the little video camera on himself. "This is Joey Bingham with an exclusive story," he said. "We have here the magician himself, the master of demons, the man responsible for the missing boy's magical disappearance."

Then Bingham crouched in front of Theopolis and aimed the camera at him.

"Mr. Theopolis," the reporter said. "Tell us: where is the boy?"

Theopolis smiled. "I can produce the boy at

any time," he said. "I am in complete control of the dimensional shift that has occurred."

"The what?" Ty said.

Theopolis fixed him with an evil glare. "The demons under my power can alter dimensions," he said in a rough whisper. "If I so desire, they will take a piece of our dimension and move it to another dimension. That is what they have done."

"And you can bring him back any time?" Charlie said.

Theopolis nodded gravely.

"Then do it," Charlie said.

Theopolis threw his head back and laughed. Bingham was getting the whole thing on video. "I will, young man," the magician said. "At tonight's performance. Then the world will see that I am the greatest—and indeed, the first ever—real, true magician in history!"

5 Proof

"This is ridiculous," Charlie said.

He and Ty were in the office behind the front desk of the Abracadabra Hotel with Annie Solo, the girl who often worked at the registration desk. She sat in the chair closest to the TV and twirled her glasses between her fingers.

Ty leaned back in the big chair in the corner. "I don't know, Hitchcock," he said. He put his hands behind his head. "Theopolis is pretty amazing. He proved he can do real magic."

"He did not," Charlie insisted.

Annie nodded. "He did," she said, still staring at the TV. The news was showing Joey Bingham's interview with Theopolis for the fifth time that afternoon. "He nailed the trapdoor shut. It had to be demons."

"Dimensional shift," Ty said.

Charlie rolled his eyes.

"I think it's real," Annie said. "I think it wasn't a trick at all. I think it was real magic. I truly believe that."

"You're crazy," Charlie said.

"I'm with Annie, Hitch," Ty said. "Am I crazy too?"

Charlie swallowed. They might be becoming friends, but Ty was still the scariest kid in eighth grade. He decided to ignore the question.

"Okay then. Prove us wrong, Charlie," Annie said.

"That's my plan," Charlie said, standing up. "Come on, Ty."

"Why should I?" Ty asked, leaning back in his chair.

"In the name of truth?" Charlie suggested. "Because uncovering mysteries in this hotel is what we do?"

Ty crossed his arms and stared at Charlie.

"Because I helped you solve two mysteries already, so you owe me?" Charlie said. He grinned sheepishly.

"He's got you there," Annie said. "Without Charlie, you'll never get that bike you've had your eye on."

Charlie smiled at Annie. The Slamhammer—which Ty was really close to being able to buy—would convince him.

"Fine," Ty said. "Where do we start?"

"Theopolis's room," Charlie said. "Let's go."

* * *

"Master Hitchcock. Master Yu. Where are you two headed?" Brack asked as Charlie and Ty stepped into his elevator.

"To see Mr. Theopolis," Charlie said.

"Thirteenth floor," Brack said. "Yes."

"It's so weird that he's on the thirteenth floor," Ty said. "No one stays on the thirteenth floor!"

"Why not?" Charlie asked as the elevator started its slow climb. "Actually," he added, "I guess I've heard that before."

"Some hotels don't even have thirteenth floors," Ty said.

"That's true," Brack said. He shrugged. "It's an old tradition, and lots of old-time magicians are very superstitious," he said. "Many of them believe that the number thirteen is a sort of bad luck number."

"Yeah," Ty said. "That's because it is."

"No, it isn't," Charlie said, rolling his eyes. "That's ridiculous. It's just a number. Numbers aren't bad luck."

"Some would disagree with you, Master Hitchcock," said Brack. "Some say the number itself has bad magic in it," he explained. He pulled out his watch again and considered it. "I always thought it had something to do with time."

He popped open the watch. "The last hour of the day is twelve," he explained, pointing at the watch face. "Perhaps a thirteenth hour seems unnatural, and so therefore the thirteenth number seems unnatural."

The old man turned to face Ty. "Have a close look," he said. He held out the watch to Ty, and Ty leaned close.

"Yup," he said. "It goes up to tw—"

But he was cut off, because suddenly a fine stream of water squirted from the center of the watch, soaking Ty's face.

"Hey!" Ty said, covering his face. "What gives?"

Charlie couldn't help laughing. "Good trick, Brack," he said. "But—I looked closely at your watch earlier today. It was definitely not a joke watch. I could tell from the shine that it was real, old metal."

"Indeed," Brack said.

He reached into the pocket of his coat and produced the real watch.

The two were nearly identical, Charlie noticed. Anyone would have been fooled.

"I had this one specially made," Brack said, "just so my two watches the real antique one and the fake, practical-joke one—would look almost exactly alike. Only an expert—or you, Mr. Hitchcock—would be able to tell them apart."

The old man giggled as the door opened on the thirteenth floor. "In fact, I've squirted my own face more than once by accident," he said. "Anyway, here you are."

"Thanks a lot, Brack," Ty said, wiping his face.

"Yeah, thanks," said Charlie, and the boys stepped out.

The hallway was completely dark. "Hey, is this right?" Charlie asked. "The lights are all off!" He turned back to the elevator, but the doors were already closed, and the elevator was already heading back down to the lobby.

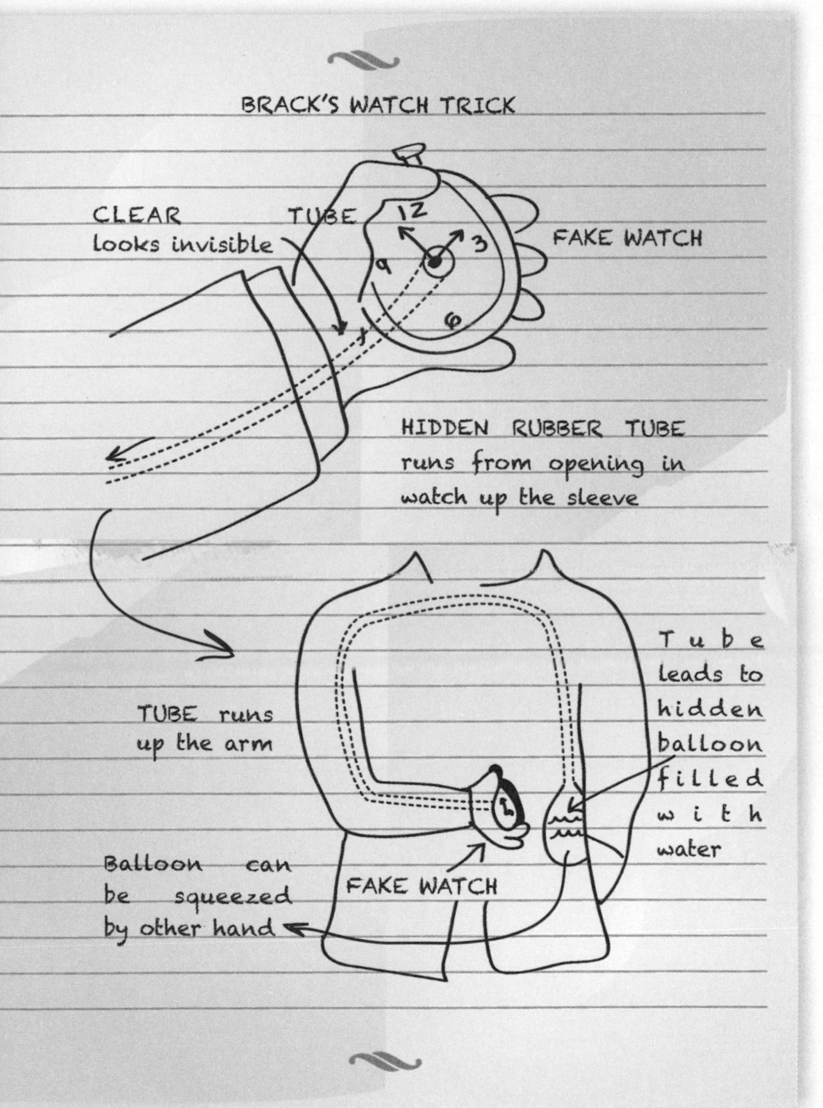
BRACK'S WATCH TRICK
CLEAR TUBE
looks invisible
12
3
9
6
FAKE WATCH
HIDDEN RUBBER TUBE
runs from opening in
watch up the sleeve
TUBE runs
up the arm
Tube
leads to
hidden
balloon
filled
with
water
Balloon can
be squeezed
by other hand
FAKE WATCH

6
Room 1307

"Let's go," Ty said. "Theopolis is in room 1305, I think."

"Isn't it weird that it's so dark here?" Charlie asked, looking down the gloomy hallway. "It feels so creepy."

1305

Ty shrugged. "Not really," he said. "I mean, no one but Theopolis is staying here."

They walked slowly down the dark hall. Only the little lights on the walls offered any light at all.

"No one else is staying on the floor?" Charlie asked.

"Nope. Theopolis requested this floor," said Ty. "Otherwise we'd never even bother offering it. Everyone insists on staying somewhere else because of the whole thirteenth floor thing. I told you. Magicians are superstitious."

"Why would Theopolis ask to stay here?" Charlie said.

"According to Annie, he said the floor has a lot of power," Ty said. "Power he would harness for his magic."

Charlie laughed. "Oh, that makes sense," he muttered.

"All right. Here we are," Ty said, stopping. "Room 1305."

Room 1305 was a corner room. Some light showed under the door. Charlie knocked.

"Mr. Theopolis?" he said.

The door swung open. "It is I!" Theopolis declared grandly. "The Great and Powerful Theopolis!" He raised his arms toward the ceiling and waited.

Ty and Charlie looked at each other.

Abruptly, Theopolis lowered his arms and looked behind them. Then he frowned. "Say, Joey Bingham, that reporter from the news show. Isn't he here with you?" he asked. The boys shook their heads.

"Oh," said the magician. Then he went to the couch and sat down. He grabbed the remote for the TV and starting clicking through the channels.

After a second, he looked back up at Charlie and Ty. "You're still here, I see. Well, come on in, then," Theopolis said. "Did you need something?"

"We were, uh, hoping to look around," Charlie said. "We, uh—"

"We work at the Abracadabra," Ty chimed in. "So, you know, we need to make sure everything's going all right. You know, with your hotel stay."

"You mean you're looking for the missing boy?" Theopolis asked, grinning a little. "Look all you want. You won't find anything. But keep it down. I'm trying to watch bowling in here."

He picked up a bowl of chips from the table and started munching away.

It didn't take long to search the suite. Charlie and Ty went over every floorboard and wall panel, looking for hidden switches and doors. They found nothing.

When they had both searched high and low, they met in the bedroom and talked quietly so that Theopolis wouldn't hear them.

"There's only one bedroom," Ty said. "Weird."

"Why is that weird?" Charlie asked quietly, so the magician wouldn't overhear.

"Well, the hotel has normal rooms, and it has suites," Ty said. "This is a suite. It has a living room, and it has a separate bedroom. But all the suites I've ever seen have two bedrooms."

"Hmm," Charlie said. "Maybe the thirteenth floor is different, and you never knew because you hardly ever come to the thirteenth floor. Since no one stays here, I mean."

"Maybe," Ty said.

Charlie and Ty headed back to the living room. "So, it seems like everything is on the up-and-up," Charlie said.

Theopolis snorted. "If you mean you didn't find the boy, I know that, of course," said the magician, munching away at his chips. "That's because he's in a magical realm right now. He's not here in the hotel."

Theopolis had his feet up on the coffee table now, so his robe was a little open at the ankles. Charlie noticed he had on a pair of jeans underneath his dark robe.

The Great and Powerful Theopolis didn't look so powerful now, lounging on his couch with potato chip crumbs on his chin.

The boys closed the door behind themselves and headed back toward the elevator.

"Well, I guess that was a waste of time," Ty said. "We didn't find any clues about the missing kid at all."

"Maybe not," Charlie said, "but it's never a waste of time to investigate every possibility."

"Wait a second," Ty said, grabbing Charlie's shirt. "Listen."

Charlie held his breath. "I don't hear anything," he whispered.

"I do," Ty said. He put his ear to the wall. "It sounds like a TV is on."

Charlie listened at the wall too. Something roared on the other side.

"Okay, now I hear it," he said. "But it's probably just Theopolis. Remember? He was watching TV in his room."

"He was watching bowling," Ty pointed out. "This sounds like . . ."

He paused, listening. Then he nodded, a smug look on his face. "Yup, it's *Alien Cyborg Attack Part Seven*. I've seen it at least a hundred times. This is the part right before the Cyborgs disembark from—"

"I believe you," Charlie said.

"So where's it coming from?" Ty asked.

Charlie looked around. He glanced up ahead at the door to room 1307. "The TV must be on in there," he said.

Then he knocked on the door. "Hello?" he called. "Anyone there? Paul?"

"There's no way any guests are staying in this room," Ty said. "Annie would have told me. Theopolis is the only guy on the floor. So whoever's in there watching the movie, it isn't a guest. I guarantee it."

"Is anyone in there?" Charlie called again.

There was no reply.

Ty and Charlie looked at each other and said at the same time, "Passkey!"

"It's in the office," Ty said as he stabbed the elevator call button. "Come on."

7 Empty

Ty twirled the key chain with the hotel passkey on it as the elevator climbed back up to the thirteenth floor. There were three of them in the elevator, but this time the third wasn't Brack.

"Thanks for letting me tag along," said Joey Bingham. "This will be quite a scoop if the missing boy is in room 1307. The whole city is talking about Theopolis's performance."

Ty tapped the golden railing inside the elevator. "I don't understand why Brack isn't in the elevator," he said. "He's always in this elevator."

There was a ding as the elevator reached the thirteenth floor. The doors opened, and the three of them stepped into the hallway.

"Hello!" a voice said. Charlie spun around and there was Brack, standing in the open doors of another elevator.

"Hello," he said, smiling. "I guess I'm not quite where you expected me to be, huh?"

"What are you up to, Brack?" Charlie said.

"Nothing, nothing," said Brack. "There's more than one elevator in this hotel. Sometimes I like to check out the others. Get a different view on things. Good luck with your case." He slipped back into his usual elevator, closed the doors, and was off.

"That was weird," Charlie said.

Ty laughed. "Brack is weird," he said.

The boys and the reporter rushed to room 1307. The sound of the movie was gone.

"Totally quiet now," Ty said as he fumbled with the passkey. He opened the door and the three of them rushed in . . .

. . . and tripped over the coffee table in the total darkness.

"Watch it!" Ty said.

"Who's on my head?" Charlie squealed.

"Get off my camera!" shouted Bingham.

Ty managed to reach a lamp and switch it on. "I'd say there's no one staying in this room," he said.

It was empty. There were no suitcases in the room, none of the towels had been used, and the beds were made. Charlie noticed there were two bedrooms in this suite, unlike Theopolis's.

Ty picked up the room phone and waited a moment. "Hey, Annie," he said. "Has anyone checked into room 1307 recently?" He didn't have to wait long for a reply.

"Thanks," he said, and hung up. "Like I said. No one. She didn't even have to look it up. No one ever stays on this floor."

"Besides Theopolis," Charlie said. "But why him?"

"Because of the power," Ty said. "Like I told you."

"Okay, okay, the power of the thirteenth floor," Charlie said, trying not to roll his eyes, "but what other normal human reason might he have?"

The reporter snapped his fingers. "No prying eyes!" he said. "And no eavesdroppers."

"Exactly what I was thinking," Charlie said. "It would be easy to hide the boy on this floor, but on another floor someone might notice."

"So let's look around," Ty said. "Maybe he

moved him, and the TV will be on in some other room."

But the three didn't make it more than few feet from 1307 before there was a great flash of light, a booming crash like thunder, and the deep evil cackle they had begun to associate with Theopolis's magic.

At the end of the hall, in front of the door to the emergency stairs and the ice machine, there appeared—in a billowing cloud of smoke—a demon.

The demon was huge and purple and muscular, with great twirling horns on its head, and huge claws and cloven feet. Its tail swung violently behind it.

"Who dares disturb Theopolis?" the demon bellowed, its voice echoing through the dark halls of the thirteenth floor.

"We're sorry!" Bingham said. He dropped to his knees and covered his face. "Please don't hurt us!"

ICE

"You must stay off this floor!" the demon shouted. The walls seemed to shake. "The thirteenth floor is rich with power, but it can destroy simple mortals like you!"

Lightning flashed through the hall. Thunder boomed. The demon roared.

Ty, Charlie, and Bingham sprinted for the elevators. They stabbed at the call button. "Come on, come on!" Ty said. "Hurry, Brack!"

But Charlie stopped. "Wait a second," he said. "What are we, little kids?" He turned and looked at the demon. It hadn't moved. It still roared and cackled. Thunder still clapped and lightning still crashed across the ceiling. "These are the same special effects Theopolis used on stage," Charlie said. "Are we going to let him scare us away so easily?"

He stomped back up the hall toward the demon. Ty and Bingham stayed behind him.

"Who dares disturb Theopolis?" the demon growled.

"That's the same thing it said before," Charlie said. "It's on a loop, I bet. If I can find the projector, I can just switch it off."

A hand clamped on his shoulder.

"Do not approach the demon!" a deep voice said. Charlie spun around and was faced by Theopolis himself.

"Didn't you hear the great beast's warning?" the magician roared. "He protects me at all costs. He is far more powerful than you could possibly imagine! You must run from this place and never come back!"

Charlie smirked at him and shrugged. Then he walked right up to the demon. He reached around in the smoke until he found a rectangular device. He found a power cord and followed it to the wall. Then he unplugged it.

The demon vanished. The smoke settled and began to dissipate. The thunder was silenced, and the lightning flashes stopped.

Charlie turned back to the hallway, holding

the end of the power cord in his hand. “How do you explain this, Theopolis?” he asked.

But there was no reply. The magician had vanished.

8 The Black Stamp

"I'm certain Paul is on the thirteenth floor someplace," Charlie said once they were back in the lobby. "It's the quietest floor on the hotel, and we heard someone watching that movie. *Space Mutant Invaders Part Ten*, or whatever."

"Ooh, I love that movie," Annie Solo said. She took a bite off her cherry licorice whip. "Remember that part when the alien with five tentacles bit the head off the—"

"That was *Space Mutant Invaders Part Four*," Ty said. "In Part Ten, it—"

"Kind of getting off track here," Charlie said. "We have a mystery to solve, remember?"

Annie shrugged. "Maybe you do," she said. "But I don't."

"You don't still think Theopolis is a real magician, do you?" Charlie asked. "Not after the special effects show we told you about in the hallway."

"Just because the big demon upstairs was fake, that doesn't mean that Paul's disappearance was fake too," Annie said.

Before Charlie could argue, Ty jumped in.

"Maybe we should take another look at that wardrobe," he said. "The one Theopolis used for the trick."

"We looked at it already," Charlie said.

"Yeah, I know," Ty said. "And you said something seemed wrong. But you never figured out what."

"It's worth a try," Charlie said.

* * *

Back under the stage, the crews were already moving things around for the evening performance.

"I hope the wardrobe is still here," Charlie said. "It'll be way trickier to sneak a look at it if it's already upstairs for the show."

Two stagehands were standing nearby. "You mean Theopolis's wardrobe? For the show?" one of them asked.

Charlie said, "That's the one. You know where it is?"

Both stagehands nodded toward the corner, where a huge shape was covered with a dark sheet. "There it is," said one of the men. "That goofball Theopolis won't let anyone move it but him or his assistants."

"That's okay with us," the other stagehand added. "That thing looks heavy."

"Yeah, it does," Charlie said.

"You kids stay away from it, got it?" the first man said. "I don't want old Theo thinking someone messed with his precious closet."

"Okay, got it," Charlie said.

Then the stagehands walked away.

As soon as the two men were gone, Charlie and Ty rushed over and pulled the sheet from the wardrobe.

"I don't know, Hitch," Ty said once Charlie had opened the wardrobe's doors. "This thing looks the same to me as it did before."

"Me too," Charlie said. He tried the false bottom, and it opened. Everything was just how he remembered it. He climbed right inside and tapped on every surface.

“What’s that?” Ty asked, pointing at a black stain on the back inner wall of the wardrobe.

Charlie squinted at the stain. “It looks printed,” he said. “I think it’s the logo and company name of the manufacturer. It says, ‘Hockney and Sons, 1935.’”

“Wow,” Ty said. “That thing is really old-time, like Brack.”

Charlie tapped his chin. “Brack . . . time . . . ” he said quietly. Ty’s words were reminding him of something. Then he snapped his fingers. “Brack’s watch! That’s it!”

"His watch?" Ty said. "The squirting one?"

Charlie nodded.

"What does that have to do with an old wardrobe under the stage?" Ty asked, looking confused.

"I have a phone call to make," Charlie said. "Come on."

9

Video Proof

"Thanks for coming down and setting this up so quickly," Charlie said. He was back in the office behind the front desk again.

Annie, Ty, and Bingham were sitting in various chairs and couches. At the front of the room, fiddling with cables and a wide-screen monitor, was Kyle Bukowski, president of the Blackstone Middle School A/V Club.

"It's no problem," Kyle said. "You know I'm always happy to help with an audio/video emergency. In a moment, I'll have all nine videos that we shot of Theopolis's performance cued up for us."

Kyle plugged in a few things, pushed a couple of buttons, and *voila*! Nine moving images popped up on the monitor, each in its own section. Each little video showed a different angle of Theopolis's performance.

They watched the whole vanishing act a couple of times.

"It's still amazing," Annie said, shaking her head. "I'm so impressed."

"What are we looking for, exactly?" Ty asked.

Charlie watched the videos until he saw just the right frame.

"Kyle, can you pause it right there," Charlie

said, "so we have a clear view of the inside of the wardrobe?"

"Sure," Kyle said. He paused one of the nine videos and then zoomed in. "How's this?"

"Perfect," Charlie said. He pointed at the inside of the wardrobe. "Anything look funny to you, Ty?"

Ty squinted at the screen. "What do you mean?" he asked.

"Look at the inside back wall," Charlie said. He leaned back in the big chair. "What's *not* there?"

Ty squinted. He leaned in closer and closer to the monitor, until his nose practically touched the screen.

Then his eyes went wide. "The black stamp!" he said.

Charlie smiled and said, "Hockney and Sons, 1935."

"How did you know that wouldn't be there?" Ty asked.

"Wait a second," said Bingham. "Who's Hockney?"

"I'll explain later," Charlie said. "First we have to find that wardrobe." He pointed at the one on the monitor.

"That's not the real wardrobe?" Annie asked.

"Nope," Charlie said. "Not at all."

"So where's the real one?" Ty said.

"Probably somewhere he could keep a close eye on it," Charlie said, "and where no one would be likely to stumble upon it."

He and Ty thought for a moment, and it came to them at the very same time.

Together they said, "The thirteenth floor!"

"But where?" Annie said, shaking her head. "You two have already checked his room, and you roamed the halls. It couldn't be another room, because he wouldn't have a key to any other rooms."

Charlie smiled at Ty. "Remember how you said every suite has at least two bedrooms?"

Charlie said. “I have a hunch about where the second bedroom in Theopolis’s room has disappeared to.”

“What are you talking about?” asked Ty.

“Before I answer that,” said Charlie, “we should go talk to Brack.”

Ty squinted at him. “You think he might have seen something?” he asked.

“Yeah, if he’s been checking out the other elevators,” Charlie said. “He might have seen a couple of men pushing a wardrobe.”

10
The Closet

The thirteenth floor was even darker and creepier than it had been earlier that day.

Demonic laughter filled the hallway. The floors creaked, even when no one was walking. Every so often, something shadowy would flicker across the hallway ahead of them—always just out of sight.

"More of Theopolis's special effects," Charlie said. "Don't let them frighten you."

"Who—who's frightened?" said Bingham.

"You are, for one," said Ty. "Here's his room."

The three of them stopped in front of room 1305. Charlie knocked. "Mr. Theopolis?" he said.

The door swung open. "What do you two want?" Theopolis said. "Haven't you harassed me enough?"

"The reporter is with us this time," Charlie said.

Theopolis's eyes lit up. "Then enter if you dare!" he shouted.

Charlie and Ty rolled their eyes, and the three visitors walked in. "Okay, Ty," said Charlie as Bingham began filming. "If this were a regular two-bedroom suite, where would the second bedroom be?"

Ty looked around, and his face wrinkled with

the strain. "I think," he said, turning slowly in the living room, "right there."

He stopped and pointed at the closet doors. They were tall and black, like the polished top keys of a piano. In fact, much of the room was decorated with the same black finish.

Charlie strode to the closet and pulled open the doors. The inside of the closet was very familiar. Bright blond wood.

"It looks just like the wardrobe," Ty said.

"Except for one thing that's missing," Charlie said. "The stamp."

"Do not go into that closet!" Theopolis bellowed. He ran and got between the boys and the closet. "There is great and terrible power in there! I can't be held responsible for what might happen!"

"Wait," Ty said. "Do you hear that? It sounds like another movie. In fact, I'm pretty sure it's *Alien Cyborg Attack Part Eight.*"

Charlie smiled. Then he walked right into

the closet. He tapped the back wall, and it instantly sprang open.

"A false back," Charlie said. "Just as I thought. And the TV we heard was coming from in here, not room 1307 at all."

Charlie stepped through the opening, right into the second bedroom. It had been hidden behind the wardrobe, and the wardrobe had been disguised as a simple closet.

"It is done," said Charlie, moving aside so that Ty and Bingham could see. "Behold!"

A young boy sat on the bed. He had a bowl of popcorn in his lap, and was staring at the TV. Sure enough, it was showing *Alien Cyborg Attack Part 8*.

"Oh, hi," the boy said.

He looked over Charlie's shoulder to see Ty and Bingham climbing into the bedroom too.

"Paul Juke!" exclaimed Ty.

"Hi, Ty. Um, is it over?" Paul asked.

"Is what over?" Bingham said.

"Well," said Paul. "The magic trick, of course."

"You're in on it?" Ty said.

"Well, yeah," said Paul. "I'm saving up for a bike, and Uncle Theo said he'd pay me."

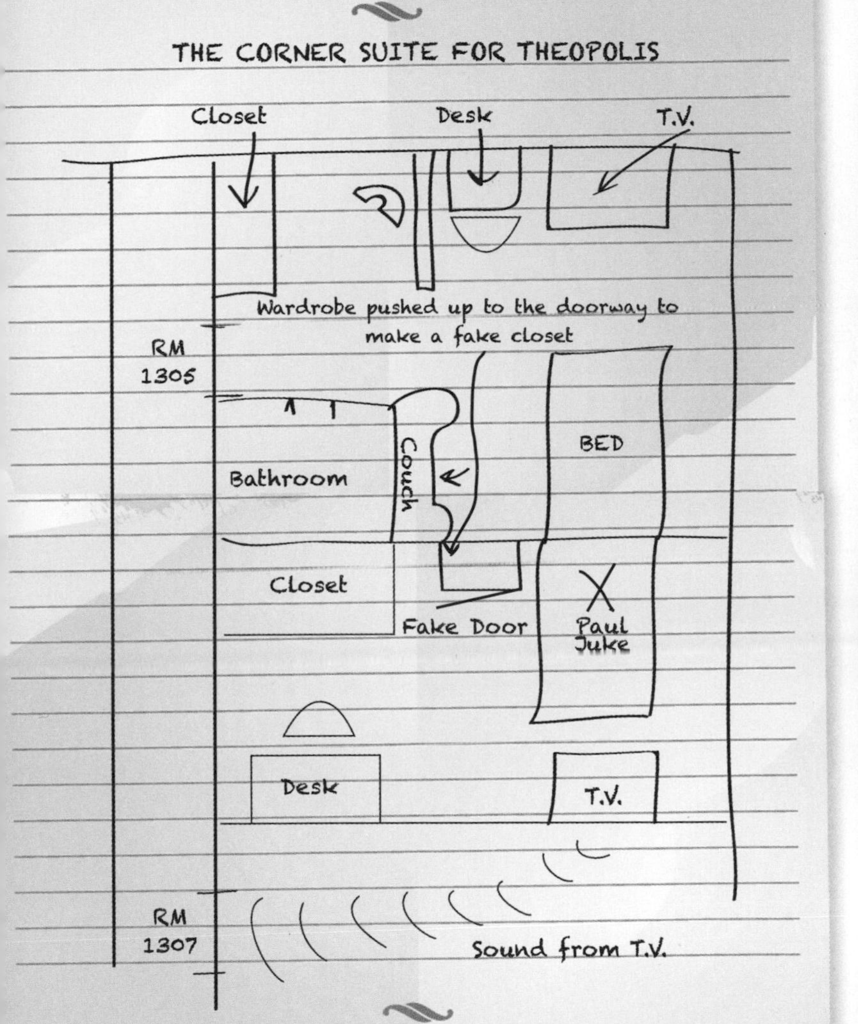
THE CORNER SUITE FOR THEOPOLIS
Closet
Desk
T.V.
Wardrobe pushed up to the doorway to make a fake closet
RM 1305
BED
Bathroom
Couch
Closet
Fake Door
Paul Juke
Desk
T.V.
RM 1307
Sound from T.V.

11 The Big Finale

"This is Joey Bingham for Action 50 news," the reporter said, grinning at his own camera. "I'm at the Abracadabra Hotel, where the great Theopolis is about to make the boy who vanished at the noon show reappear."

The house was packed. Everyone who had gone to the noon show was back, and so were loads of people who had seen Bingham's earlier reports about the missing boy.

"Are you sure about this?" Charlie whispered. He sat with Ty on an overturned crate under the stage. They were going to help with the big finish Theopolis had promised. "We can still reveal the truth. We figured out that Theopolis isn't a true magician, like he claims."

"We could do that," Ty said. "We could also enjoy all the publicity for this show, for the hotel, and for the theater. This is going to do wonders for the Abracadabra Hotel. Besides, you convinced me and Annie, right? And that was the point."

Charlie nodded. Just then, one of the stage-hands popped his head in the door. "Everyone ready down here?" he said. "Did you get the nails out of the trapdoor?"

"Yep. We're ready," replied Ty.

Paul got up from his seat against the wall. "Finally," he said. He stepped up on the crate between Ty and Charlie and added, "Can't wait to get my new bike. My uncle owes me big time."

Charlie and Ty stood and clasped their hands together. "Ready?" said Ty.

"Ready," said Paul.

"One," they all said together, "two, three!" And with a great grunt, Paul was launched up and through the open trapdoor, into the wardrobe on the stage—the original wardrobe, with the false bottom and stamp that said "Hockney and Sons, 1935."

Charlie and Ty sat back down and waited. Seconds later, they heard the crowd above burst into cheers and applause.

"I guess it went well," Charlie said.

"And you know what it means when the hotel does well, and I've helped," said Ty.

Charlie nodded. "Yup," he said.

"A raise," said Ty. "And soon Paul won't be

the only one with a new bike. Any money I make brings me one step closer to my Tezuki Slamhammer 750, Edition 6, in cherry-pop lightning red."

"I guess when you get the bike you won't need my help anymore," Charlie said. "Right?"

Ty shrugged. "I don't know," he said. "I mean, there's always a new mystery at the Abracadabra."

"Which reminds me," Charlie said. "Isn't Brack planning another huge magic show?"

"Indeed I am," a voice said. But when the boys turned to look, Brack was nowhere to be found.

12

An Announcement

Exactly one week later, Charlie and Ty stood inside the front doors of the Abracadabra Hotel. The lobby was more crowded than it had been in decades.

"Wow," said Charlie. "What's going on?"

As a permanent resident of the hotel, Ty should know why the place was packed. But the big guy just shrugged.

"Beats me," he said. "I'll try to find my mom."

"In this craziness?" Charlie said.

While Ty weaved through the crowd to try to reach the registration desk, Charlie tried snooping around. He slipped behind a big marble column and listened to a few people talking.

"Any idea what the big news is?" said a woman in a suit.

"Nope," a man replied. He had a camera around his neck. "We got a call at the paper this morning, and I came right down."

Another man walked up in a hurry. "They're calling us in," he said, out of breath. "Come on. Let's get a seat in front if we can."

The three people ran off toward the dining room off the lobby. "Reporters," Charlie said to himself.

The crowd in the lobby streamed toward the

dining room. Charlie spotted a bunch of other people who must be reporters. The rest of them seemed like they might be magicians.

"I can't find my mom anywhere," said Ty, walking up to Charlie. "I don't know what's going on."

"Well, whatever's going on," Charlie said, "it's going on in there." He pointed to the dining room.

"Then let's go," said Ty. The boys hurried in just before the doors were closed.

The tables had been cleared away. At the front of the big room was a stage. A microphone stood in the center.

Hundreds of chairs had been set up. Reporters and photographers filled the chairs and lined the walls and aisles too. Men and women in tuxedoes and colorful clothes and jester costumes were also sprinkled through the crowd. Ty and Charlie could barely fit in the room.

"I guess they're waiting for someone to give

a speech," Charlie whispered. "How did they all find out about this?" he asked Ty.

"This must be how," Ty said. He bent over and grabbed a sheet of paper from the carpeted floor.

Just then, the lights dimmed in the dining room and a spotlight shined on the lectern. "Here goes," said Charlie.

And it was just as he suspected. From the side door next to the little stage, out came Brack, the elevator operator of the hotel. Secretly, Brack was Abracadabra himself: the founder and owner of the hotel. But only Charlie knew that.

"What's he doing?" Ty said.

"Thank you all for coming," said Brack, smiling at the crowd. "I'm sure you're wondering why I've called you all here this morning," he said.

A reporter in the front raised his hand and shouted, "*You* called us? We thought it was something important."

"Yeah!" someone else called out. "You're just the elevator man!"

"Ah," said Brack. He removed his hat. "That is what I've come to talk to you about. I am not just the elevator operator."

"He also scrubs the toilets," joked a magician along the wall. Charlie scowled.

Brack cleared his throat at the microphone. Then he raised both hands in a high, wide arc over his head. He threw back his head and shouted, "Abracadabra!"

A great puff of smoke came up from the stage floor. The lights flickered and flashed in the dining room. When the smoke cleared, Brack was gone.

A moment later, the lights flashed on for a second. Thunder crashed through the room. The walls and chairs shook. And then, from the high ceiling over the stage, smoke and light fell. Then came a man. He wore a red and green robe and a shining silver crown set in a big colorful turban.

As his feet touched the stage, he raised his arms and smiled.

"I am Brack," he announced, "and I am Abracadabra! Be here one week from tonight for my first show in fifty years—and my last!"

Thunder clapped again. Lightning flashed across the ceiling. The crowd gasped.

Flashes went off. Hands went into the air. Frenzied reporters shouted out questions and demands. Magicians rushed the stage.

The place went, in a word, nuts.

* * *

It was an hour before the dining room and lobby were cleared out. While they waited for the craziness to die down, Charlie and Ty sat on one of the red velvet couches near the front desk.

"I can't believe it," Ty said.

Charlie grinned. "I kind of already knew," he said.

Ty stared at him. "You're kidding me," he said.

"Nope," Charlie said. "I figured it out, and

Brack confirmed it." He reached into his pocket and pulled out his golden ticket. "And I'm invited to the final performance."

Ty narrowed his eyes. "I better be too," he muttered.

"I'm sure I can bring a guest," Charlie said, and winked.

13 The Little Golden Key

Many of the magicians who attended the announcement had decided to get a room at the hotel. The line to check in was getting long.

Just then, a big group of reporters came shuffling across the lobby. The reporters were moving in a tight group, and they were shouting questions.

"I think they have Brack," said Ty.

The group of reporters moved right at the boys. Soon it engulfed them.

"What tricks will you do?" one reporter shouted.

"Oh," said Brack when he saw Charlie and Ty. Brack was in his elevator operator uniform again. His face showed the stress his announcement had created. "Hello, you two," he said.

"Why have you been in hiding?" another reporter said.

"*Where* have you been hiding?" one more asked. Ty rolled his eyes.

"What's going on?" Charlie asked Brack. He had to shout to be heard over the gaggle of reporters. He struggled to shuffle along inside the ambling crowd.

"Why are you retiring from magic, after being gone all these years?" said another reporter.

"Follow my lead," Brack muttered to Charlie and Ty. He shuffled off in a new direction and the crowd followed. Ty and Charlie shuffled along with him.

"He's heading for the elevator," Ty muttered to Charlie.

Ty was right. When they got very close to the elevator bank, Brack put a hand on the boys' collars, stepped backward into the open elevator, and then quickly closed the doors. The reporters were stuck on the other side.

"Whew," Brack said, taking off his hat. "I knew this would cause a ruckus, but I wasn't prepared for so much attention." He shook his head slowly.

He pulled keys from his pocket—he had a lot of keys—and flipped through them until he found a very small golden one. Then he opened a tiny door on the elevator control panel.

"I never noticed that before," Ty said.

Inside the little door was a keyhole. Brack

used his little golden key, turned it to the right, and the elevator started going up.

"A secret floor," said Ty in a hushed, awed voice.

He looked over at Charlie and narrowed his eyes. "Did you know about this?" he asked.

Charlie glanced at Brack, who had a twinkle in his eye.

"Uh, yeah," Charlie said.

"I can't believe it, Hitch," Ty said. "I can't believe it!"

For a second, Charlie saw a glimmer of the old Ty—the biggest bully in school, not his friend.

But then Brack said, calmly, "I asked Master Hitchcock to not say anything to you, Master Yu. I wanted to tell you myself, you see. The problem was, time ran out. I'm very sorry."

"Oh, that's okay, Brack," Ty said. "I get it." He narrowed his eyes at Charlie again, but the angry look was gone.

The elevator climbed and climbed. The dial above the door swung slowly, higher and higher. It went past the top floor and kept going.

Ty looked at Brack quizzically, but he just smiled and watched the dial climb.

Finally, the elevator stopped. A bell dinged. The doors slid open.

"Whoa," said Ty. He stood there, dumbfounded, as Brack and Charlie stepped out. Before them was Brack's house on the roof.

"Pretty cool, huh?" Charlie whispered as

Ty walked slowly out of the elevator, looking around.

"Uh, yeah," Ty said. "I can't believe I never knew this was here."

"Welcome to my home," Brack said. He walked up the front path toward the big wooden doors of the mansion. "Please, follow me."

Inside, Brack headed straight to the kitchen, a sunny room at the back of the house. "Have a seat, you two," he said. "We've a lot to discuss."

"What's on your mind, Brack?" Ty said. He flipped around a chair and sat down. "Should we call you Abracadabra now?"

Brack laughed. "Don't be silly," he said. "Why, if anyone calls me Abracadabra, I'll know to keep my guard up."

"What do you mean?" Charlie asked as he sat down at the table.

Brack sighed and sipped his tea. "For a long time," he said, "I was the most famous magician in the city, maybe in the country."

"Pff," said Ty. "You were the biggest magician in the world, probably ever."

"Perhaps," said Brack. "When I founded this hotel, I became quite an attraction. That much is certain. For many years, young magicians from all over the world wanted to share the stage with me."

"Sure," Charlie said. "Who wouldn't?"

Brack nodded. "At first, I was honored," he said. "But then it became clear: most of those young magicians were just looking to grab their own piece of fame. They didn't respect me. They didn't care about me at all."

"Harsh," said Ty.

"Indeed, it wasn't long before a new breed of magician began showing up, right here at the hotel," said Brack. "These were true cutthroats. If it would help their careers to take me down a notch, or eliminate me entirely, all the better. They'd stop at nothing to achieve their greedy goals."

"Whoa," Ty whispered.

"At first I tried to help," Brack went on. "Soon it became overwhelming. So many tried to take advantage of me, or even try to put me down or set me up for failure. Then I realized I could so easily just disappear."

"Poof!" Ty said. He snapped his fingers.

Brack chuckled. "Not quite like that," he said. "That's how I would have done it in a magic show, of course. In a grand puff of smoke, like at this morning's press conference. But I had something different in mind."

"So you became Brack," Charlie said. "The mild-mannered, easy-going, hotel elevator operator."

"Precisely," Brack said. He frowned. "Now that I'm back, those fame-hungry magicians will begin hounding me at any moment. This time, I'm ready for them."

He lifted a card from the table and passed it to Ty.

"Here you are. I sent these out yesterday," Brack said. "Every magician in the country will be getting his or her invitation to my party today."

Ty looked at Brack, his eyes wide. "You're inviting them?" he said. "I thought you didn't want to see these people!"

"Oh, I can't stop them from showing up," Brack said. "But this way, I will have the upper hand in two ways."

"Which ways?" Charlie asked.

"One, they will all be here at once," Brack said. "They'll spend all their time trying to impress each other and knock each other down. They won't pester me."

"And two?" Charlie said.

"Ah," said Brack, smiling. "That's where you boys come in."

Ty and Charlie leaned forward.

"The party is tomorrow night," Brack said. "And you're both very important parts of it."

"Us?" said Charlie. "But . . . we're not magicians."

"Indeed," said Brack. He stood up and brought his teacup to the sink. "That's why I know I can count on you two to keep an eye on everyone else."

14

Filthy with Magicians

The next twenty-four hours were a flurry of activity in the hotel. Many magicians had already checked in. Now that the invitations had arrived, the magical guests gabbed and gossiped in the lobby for hours at a time. They had lunch in the hotel restaurant. They milled around the hotel games room, chatting about which tricks they'd show off at the party.

Meanwhile, the reporters were back. Word had gotten out, and it seemed like a big scoop.

The biggest scoop was Abracadabra's performance at the magic show. There was little doubt among the reporters that he had some new amazing tricks up his silk sleeves.

One reporter in particular hung around the lobby a lot—usually right next to Charlie.

"But how did you know Brack the elevator operator was actually Abracadabra?" said Joey Bingham.

It was early Sunday morning. The party was that night, and there was a lot of work to do.

"I told you, Joey," Charlie said. "I figured it out."

Joey shook his head. "I find it hard to believe," he said, "that you two would figure out this great secret."

"Why?" said Ty. "We're smart. I happen to be very intelligent, and Charlie is a total whiz at remembering stuff and figuring stuff out."

Joey smirked. "Of course you are," he said. He leaned close to the boys and said in a whisper, "But the rest of us are professional reporters. We investigate and discover secrets for a living."

"You couldn't find the missing boy," Charlie said quickly.

Joey's face went red. "I would have," he said. "Eventually."

"Anyway, we have to help Mr. Abracadabra set up for the party," said Ty. He grabbed Charlie's arm to pull him away. "We're his friends, you know."

Joey Bingham sneered as they walked off. Then he gasped—loudly—at something behind them.

The rest of the lobby—full of magicians and reporters—gasped too. Ty and Charlie turned and saw flashes go off. The reporters began to

run for the front door as it swung closed. There, smiling and flourishing for the hundreds of cameras on him, stood the Great Theopolis.

Joey ran toward the door with the others. Charlie and Ty stayed back to watch. They leaned against the registration desk. Annie leaned on the desk from the other side.

"I thought he checked out," Charlie said.

Annie said, "He did. I guess he's back. He'll want his room on the thirteenth floor again, I guess." She started shuffling through the room cards and keys. "He always stays there."

"He was probably invited to the big party," said Charlie.

Ty nodded. "And after his big stunt with the disappearing kid last week at the show," he said, "Theopolis is the most famous magician in town."

"He *was* the most famous magician in town, you mean," said Charlie with a smirk. "Now Brack is."

"Yeah!" Annie said.

"And I bet Theopolis isn't too happy about that," Ty said. "We'll have to keep a close eye on him."

* * *

Theopolis and Joey Bingham weren't the only familiar faces to arrive at the Abracadabra Hotel that day.

Charlie also spotted Professor Pontificate, the mind-reader and hypnotist, strolling around the lobby. And, he saw, there was Mr. Madagascar, a master of levitation and long-time resident of the hotel who hardly ever left his room. Today, though, Mr. M. was in the lobby with the rest of the crowd. So was his friend Dotty Drake. She'd been a great magician's assistant in the old days.

Then there was Madame Krzyscky, the fire-eater from the theater's premier show the week before. She wore a glittery skin-tight costume in red, orange, and yellow. She looked like fire herself as she walked around the lobby.

Ty elbowed Charlie in the side and pointed across the lobby. Charlie's eyes went wide. Objects were flying through the air over the heads of the crowd in the lobby. He saw a bowling pin. He saw a baseball, a basketball, and a tennis racquet. He gasped when he saw a flaming stick, and then another.

Finally the objects stopped flying. A few people—reporters, mostly—applauded. The crowd parted and Charlie could see now: it was Mr. Thursday, master juggler.

A few weeks earlier, Charlie and Ty had thought Mr. Thursday was a ghost.

He'd been practicing his routine for a big comeback show in the hotel's old theater. Little did they know then that the magicians were running a kind of dress rehearsal for the big reappearance of Abracadabra.

"I guess everyone's here," said Ty.

Charlie looked around the lobby.

There were other jugglers.

There were jesters.

There were magicians' assistants—mostly women, but some men—of all ages, wearing leotards or long white gowns or silver sequined bodysuits.

There were plenty of men in tuxedoes and top hats, sometimes even with bunnies popping out of them.

There were all sorts of card tricks going on.

There were even people floating up near the ceiling, showing off their levitation skills.

The place was absolutely filthy with magicians.

"And just think," Charlie said. He crossed his arms. "Each and every one of them will be at Brack's party tonight."

15

Brack's Party

It was a warm evening, so most of the party-goers stayed outside. They sat on the benches in the rooftop garden. They lounged on the chairs next to the rooftop pool.

At first, no one paid much attention to Brack, all alone in his simple brown suit. Charlie and Ty stood nearby, so they could keep an eye on him. But before long, he'd been spotted, sitting at a table under a canopy.

"Hey, there's the old master!" said a magician. Everyone looked, and it only took a few short seconds before Brack's table was completely mobbed.

Magicians stood in front of his table, showing off their abilities. They made things disappear. They made things appear. They juggled. They levitated objects and levitated themselves. The assistants performed flourishes or little spins, showing off their clothes or hair or smile.

At the table, Brack smiled politely.

"Do you have an open slot in your farewell show, Mr. Abracadabra?" asked a woman who had just made her sister disappear—and then reappear as her brother.

"Please, Mr. Abracadabra," said a man as he

juggled five bowling balls while riding a unicycle, "make room for me on that stage!"

Brack didn't respond to anyone. He just smiled.

Theopolis was the last magician to arrive. He strode off the elevator and right up the front path. Then he stomped to the front of the line of magicians.

Tonight he wore his most impressive garb: a heavy black robe that shined like silk, trimmed with silver and gold thread. He carried a staff, like some ancient wizard. On each side of him were assistants, both hobbled and bent. The assistants were dressed in burlap cloaks.

Charlie elbowed Ty, who was busy watching some jugglers practicing next to the pool.

"Look who's here," Charlie said.

Theopolis threw back the hood of his robe. At the same moment, a bolt of lightning—one of Theopolis's special effects—struck his wizard's staff. Smoke rose up from his feet.

"Wow," said Ty. "You have to admit, he knows how to make an entrance."

"Mr. Abracadabra!" Theopolis said in his deepest voice. "I—the Great and Powerful Theopolis, lord of the demon realm and the greatest sorcerer in this dimension—have come to offer a challenge."

Brack winked at Ty and Charlie. Then he looked back at Theopolis. "Go on," he said.

A few people nearby chuckled. Theopolis ignored them. "This hotel has become old," Theopolis said, grandly raising his arms. "You have become old."

Brack shrugged and smiled. "Too true," he said.

"Your retirement from magic," said Theopolis, "draws near. You will no doubt enjoy a rest. It will do you good."

"He's been resting for fifty years," Ty whispered to Charlie.

"The hotel itself could use some fixing too," Theopolis went on. "Its age is showing, as yours is. It needs to be . . . updated. Brought up to modern times. You've been in hiding for a long time, old man. The world has changed, and so has magic."

"Perhaps," said Brack.

"And so, I offer this challenge," Theopolis said. "I will now perform an act of magic so striking, so amazing, that you will not believe it possible."

"An illusion?" Brack said.

"No illusion," said Theopolis. "True magic—the demonic power I learned in my studies. Power from other dimensions."

"I see," said Brack. "Then what is the challenge?"

"I say it is magic," Theopolis said. "You say it is an illusion. Then prove it. After the feat, you will have until the night of your final performance to show how it was done."

"And if I can't?" Brack said.

"Ah," said Theopolis. He grinned and made a steeple of his fingers before his face. "If you cannot, then you back out of your final performance and hand the theater over to me . . . and the hotel along with it."

16
True Magic

"What?!" said Charlie.

"That's ridiculous!" shouted Ty.

Brack put up his hand to silence the boys. "What if I do show how it was done?" Brack asked Theopolis. "What will you give me?"

Theopolis frowned in disdain. “It’s barely worth considering,” he said, “but if that happens, which I very much doubt, I suppose we can work together to reach some sort of . . . monetary agreement.”

“No money,” Brack said. “You will agree never to step foot inside this hotel again.”

“Very well,” said Theopolis. He bowed deeply.

Brack stood up from his chair and walked out from behind the table. He didn’t look like the old elevator operator today. He didn’t look old at all, except in the way that a tall and mighty oak tree looks old.

Brack stood in front of Theopolis. They were about the same height when Brack stood fully upright.

“Begin your trick, Theo,” Brack said. He didn’t smile.

“It’s no trick,” said Theopolis.

“Yes, yes,” Brack said. “It’s true magic. Just get on with it.”

Theopolis bowed deeply, smiling. With a flourish of his black robe, he walked to the far side of the pool. He pushed roughly through the gathering crowds.

For a moment, Charlie lost sight of the magician. Then Theopolis reappeared at the edge of the pool. He walked to the end of the diving board and stopped.

Ty and Charlie shuffled over to stand with Brack. "You boys watch closely," Brack said out of the side of his mouth. "You can bet Theopolis won't make this easy."

Charlie nodded. But he wasn't worried. He and Ty had solved one of Theopolis's tricks before. Maybe this wouldn't be so hard.

* * *

Any hopes Charlie and Ty had that this trick would be as simple as Theopolis's last one were dashed right away.

Theopolis was in prime form. Thick white smoke rose up from the ground and settled over the roof.

Theopolis threw back his head and raised his staff with both hands. Thunder clapped across the sky. Party guests flinched and ran for cover under canopies and on the mansion's big front porch.

Only Brack, Charlie, and Ty stayed beside the pool.

The whole rooftop estate filled with an eerie red light. The light crackled and popped, like tiny bolts of lightning.

"Great demons of the dimensions of power!" Theopolis shouted up at the thundering red sky. "I call upon you! Bestow upon me your darkest power!"

As he spoke, the thunder grew louder. The sky became a deeper, darker red. The lights at the party—which had been so bright and friendly—switched off.

Suddenly the rooftop party looked less like a celebration of Abracadabra's return, and more like a vision from a nightmare.

"Give me the power!" Theopolis screamed at the sky once more.

Then—slowly at first—he rose from the diving board. He kept his head and arms up to the sky, as he rose higher and higher, until he was at least twenty feet over the pool.

Magicians gasped and muttered. Assistants sighed and clapped. Charlie and Tyler looked at each other, and then stared back at Theopolis.

But Theopolis wasn't done yet.

High above the rooftop, the robed figure floated farther out over the pool. He brought down the staff and lowered his head for a moment.

The crowd hushed.

Suddenly, Theopolis threw the staff straight up into the dark red sky and the white clouds of smoke and the streaks of lightning.

Charlie knew that all of it—the smoke, the thunder, the lightning—was just special effects. Still, he couldn't help being impressed. Theopolis might be a fame-hungry, underhanded jerk, but he was good at putting on a show.

The staff reached its apex and seemed to explode. When it fell back toward Theopolis—who was still floating high above the swimming pool—it was in three pieces.

The Great Theopolis didn't flinch. He caught the three pieces and immediately tossed them up. Before Charlie could guess what had happened, Theopolis was juggling the three pieces perfectly.

The crowd cheered. Brack nodded, impressed. Ty leaned closer to Charlie and whispered, "Since when does Theopolis juggle?"

Charlie shrugged. It was a good question.

Finally, Theopolis caught all three pieces at once. The staff seemed to reassemble itself. He held it aloft once more.

"I thank you, great demons of my dimension!" he shouted into the clouds. "And now, go back to your own realm!"

Lightning cracked. The thunder boomed its loudest crash yet. Charlie had to cover his ears with his hands. The red light flashed brightly, and Charlie had to turn away and close his eyes.

When Charlie looked back, Theopolis was gone.

17
Stumped

"Where'd he go?" someone shouted.

Chattering spread through the crowd of magicians and assistants. Most of them sounded very impressed. A few magicians standing near Brack and the boys said things like, "Pff, I could do that," and, "That wasn't much of a trick," and, "I don't see what the big deal is."

But it *was* a big deal, Charlie knew. Theopolis had levitated, called demons from another dimension, controlled the weather, and vanished. He'd even juggled.

Brack put his arms around Ty and Charlie.

"I hope you boys were watching closely," he said quietly. "I'll need your help to figure this one out."

Just then, someone stepped up behind them.

"Counting on the help of two children?" said Theopolis. He laughed. "This proves it. You are too old, too out of touch with magic today."

Brack didn't respond.

"You have less than one week," Theopolis said. "Then you will vacate the theater, cancel your farewell show, and hand over this hotel—and this rooftop estate—to me."

He pulled up his hood, sneered at Charlie and Ty, and stormed for the exit.

THEOPOLIS'S TRICK
THEOPOLIS levitating
and juggling
Pool

"What a nasty man," Charlie said.

Brack nodded. "Indeed," he said, "but he is also a master illusionist."

"What are you saying?" Ty asked.

"I'm saying that I hope you two have some ideas," Brack said, "because frankly, I'm stumped."

With that, the old magician walked back to his table under the canopy. None of the other magicians went over to him. They just sipped their drinks, nibbled their snacks, and talked quietly to each other about how amazing Theopolis's trick was.

18
Full Reboot

The next day was Monday, so Charlie and Ty had to get back to school. Charlie had a load of homework he hadn't done over the weekend, so for the next two days, he was stuck at home after school. He didn't get back to the hotel until Wednesday afternoon.

"Have you figured anything out?" Charlie asked Ty when he arrived at the Abracadabra.

"Of course not," Ty said. He was lounging on the couch nearest the front desk. He nodded toward the elevators.

Charlie turned to look. There was Brack—back in his elevator operator uniform—sitting in his chair in the lobby right by the elevators. He didn't look happy.

"He's been like that since the party, pretty much," Ty said. "I think he's just hoping Theopolis will let him stay on as elevator operator when he gives him the hotel."

Charlie shook his head sadly. "He's really given up already?" he asked.

"Can you blame him?" Ty said.

Just then, the front doors of the hotel swung open and Theopolis entered.

And so did a lot of other people.

Charlie recognized some of the assistants from the party. They trailed close behind him.

There were a few magicians from the party too, including Mr. Thursday, the juggling expert.

And behind the whole group of magic people were reporters. They barked questions and took photos and shot video.

Theopolis led the little parade, his face full of pride. When he reached the center of the lobby—where he could be easily seen by everyone, including Brack—he stopped.

"Ladies and gentlemen," Theopolis said, smiling smugly, "I will answer all your questions. Now, who is first?"

Joey Bingham stepped up and held out his microphone. "What are your plans for the hotel when you take it over?" he asked.

"See?" said Ty quietly to Charlie. "Everyone's acting like Brack's already lost."

Theopolis made a big show of looking up and around the lobby. "So much wasted space," he said. Then he ran a finger along the back of a nearby lobby chair. "And everything is so old."

He pretended his finger was dirty just from having rubbed the chair. The reporters gathered around him chuckled.

Charlie glanced at Brack. The old magician hung his head.

"My plan is a full reboot, if you follow me," Theopolis said. He walked toward the elevators as he spoke. "I will modernize everything. There will be projectors and flat-panel screens all over the lobby. There will be a complete staff change, naturally."

"Naturally," grunted Ty sarcastically.

"We'll start by tearing up the old theater," Theopolis said, just as he and his group reached the elevators. "Now excuse me. I will go up to my room."

Without even looking at Brack, he barked out, "Thirteenth floor, please, old man." Then he stepped into the elevator with his two hobbled assistants. Brack got up with a sigh and stepped into the elevator too. The doors closed.

Charlie gritted his teeth. "It's time for us to get to work," he said.

Ty nodded. "Where do we start?"

"First, we talk to Rocky," Charlie said.

"He's in the office," Ty said, slipping behind the front desk. "Come on."

Charlie followed. Soon the two boys were sitting in the main office. Rocky, the hotel's bellhop, leaned on a file cabinet in the corner.

"So," Charlie said, "are you with us?"

"Sure," said Rocky. "I don't want Brack to lose the hotel either. Can you imagine working for that nut Theopolis? No way. So, how can I help?"

"Give us a list of every magician who checked into the hotel since Brack's press conference," Charlie said.

"Why do we want that?" Ty asked.

"They were all at the party," Charlie said, "and they're all experts in magic, to some degree. Maybe one of them can help us."

"Coming right up," Rocky said. He went to the front desk and started tapping at the computer.

"What if they won't help us?" Ty said.

Charlie thought about it. "I don't know," he said, "but right now, what else can we do?"

19

The Best Juggler Around

Ty and Charlie talked to magicians all afternoon and into the evening. Charlie had to call home and tell his parents he'd miss dinner.

It was late when they got to Mr. Thursday, the juggler, and they weren't even halfway down the list yet.

Ty knocked on the door of room 1001. The juggler opened the door immediately.

"Yes?" he said. "Oh, it's you two. Come on in." He moved back inside and left the door open for them.

Charlie looked around. The room was a mess, strewn with bowling pins and bowling balls, softballs and baseballs, unlit torches, knives and batons. "I hope we're not bothering you," Charlie said.

"Oh, no," Mr. Thursday replied. "I was just in the middle of practicing. I'm always in the middle of practicing, actually."

"We won't take up too much of your time," Charlie said. "We're asking everyone who was at the party if they had thoughts about Theopolis's big trick."

"Helping out old man Brack, huh?" Mr. Thursday said. He sat down on the couch and crossed his legs.

"We're trying to," Ty said. He sat down

too. "We've already talked to, like, a hundred magicians."

"Well, maybe ten," Charlie said.

"Whatever," said Ty. "The point is we still have no idea how Theopolis did that stuff."

Mr. Thursday's eyebrows went up. "No idea at all?" he said.

Charlie shook his head.

"Well, the juggling was very good," Mr. Thursday said. "In fact, it was some of the best juggling I've ever seen in my life."

"Really?" said Ty. "That's surprising to hear. You're the best juggler around. I wouldn't think you'd be so quick to praise Theopolis. Is he a friend of yours?"

"Of course not," Thursday said with a chuckle. "I've never even talked to him. I just think his juggling performance was very good."

"Especially since he was floating in midair," added Charlie.

Mr. Thursday stood up. "I don't know

anything about that," he said. "I'm no levitation expert."

He moved toward the door. "Now, if you two will excuse me," he said. "I have a lot of practicing to do."

Ty stood up. "Do you have a performance coming up?" he asked.

"If everything goes according to plan," Mr. Thursday said, "yes."

Charlie and Ty stepped into the hallway. Mr. Thursday closed the door.

Ty sighed. "That was no help at all," he said, glancing at the list. "Let's see, who's next?"

Charlie yawned. "I have to get home," he said. "Let's pick this up tomorrow after school."

"Okay," said Ty. "Three o'clock. Don't be late."

20

Slamhammer!

The next day of school was the longest Charlie had ever experienced. As soon as the last bell rang, he hurried to the hotel.

Ty was already there. “Finally,” said the bigger boy when Charlie ran into the lobby, out of breath. “What took you so long?”

"How . . . how did you get here so fast?" Charlie said.

Ty laughed. "Take a guess," he said. "What's quicker than walking? In fact, what's as fast as . . . lightning?"

Charlie gasped. "You got it?" he said. "You got your bike?"

Grinning, Ty pulled it out from behind the front desk: the Tezuki Slamhammer 750, Edition 6, in cherry-pop lightning red.

"That's amazing," Charlie said, staring at the beautiful bike. "Nice work."

"Okay," said Ty. "Enough ogling. Let's get started."

Mr. Madagascar frowned when he opened the door. "What do you two want?" he said. He was in a nice emerald-green suit, but his room was a complete mess. There were at least a dozen mirrors of all sizes leaning against the walls and furniture.

"Were you at the party the other night?" Ty asked. "The one at Brack's rooftop estate, upstairs."

"Of course I was," Mr. M. said. "Every magician in the city was there."

"Did you see the trick?" Charlie asked.

"Theopolis's magic?" Mr. Madagascar said. He leaned on the open doorway.

He hasn't invited us in, Charlie thought.

"Yes, I saw it," Mr. M. said. "It was very impressive, wasn't it? The levitation was very good. Over water? Difficult business. But you two wouldn't understand."

"That good, huh?" Charlie said. "I didn't know Theopolis was an expert in levitation."

Mr. Madagascar squinted at the boy. "Yes," he said slowly, in a very rough voice. "I didn't know either."

"But you were impressed?" Charlie asked.

"Quite," said Mr. Madagascar.

Just then, someone cleared their throat behind the boys, and Charlie spun to see. It was Dotty Drake, Mr. Madagascar's assistant.

Mr. Madagascar looked at the boys. "Now you'll have to excuse us. Dotty and I are about to rehearse our act."

"Do you have a show soon?" Charlie asked.

"Ah, nothing scheduled yet, exactly," Madagascar said. "But we're very hopeful."

Then Dotty closed the door in their faces.

Four Magicians in One

The boys spent the rest of the afternoon and evening talking to other magicians. No one was especially helpful. It was nearly eight before they gave up for the night.

Charlie leaned against the front desk and yawned. "I guess I better get home," he said.

Tyler nodded. "We only have a couple more days," he said. "I'm losing hope."

Just then, Brack stepped out of the elevator and plodded across the lobby.

"Brack!" Charlie and Ty shouted. They ran over to him.

"Where have you been?" Charlie asked. "We've hardly seen you since the party."

Brack looked tired. He sat down on a bench and considered the boys. "I've been hard at work," he said.

"Rehearsing for the big farewell show?" Ty asked.

Brack sighed. "Why waste my time with that?" he said. "If I lose this bet, there won't be a farewell show." He put his hands on his knees and sat up straighter. "No," he said, "I've been trying to duplicate Theopolis's trick."

"Any luck?" Charlie said. "We could use your insight."

"Put it this way," Brack said, smiling. "I'm wearing my elevator operator outfit because all my other clothes are upstairs hanging out to dry."

"Fell in the pool a few times?" Ty said.

"Try ten times," Brack said. He chuckled. "I'll miss this place."

Charlie put a hand on Brack's shoulder. "We'll figure it out, Mr. Abracadabra," he said. "I promise."

But Brack didn't seem to be listening. He shook his head sadly. "I just can't figure it out," he said. "Juggling, levitation, special effects, vanishing . . . it's like four magicians rolled into one."

He sighed. Then he got up and headed for the break room.

22 Pale in Comparison

Charlie hardly slept for the next two nights. On Saturday, he knew he should go down to the Abracadabra Hotel for some last-minute investigating, but he couldn't bear to.

There's no point, Charlie thought. *I might as well stay in bed and watch TV all day.*

But that evening, the phone rang. It was Ty.

"Why aren't you here?" Ty said.

"Why should I be?" Charlie said. "It's over. Theopolis won. Even Brack can't figure out that crazy trick."

"Don't be such a wuss," Ty said. "Besides, I *have* figured it out."

Charlie sat up and pushed the blanket to the floor. "What do you mean?" he asked.

"It was something Brack said last night, right before you left," Ty said. "Four magicians rolled into one."

Charlie scratched his head. "What do you mean?" he asked.

"I'll explain when you get down here," Ty said, and he hung up.

* * *

Charlie was dressed and heading for the hotel in no time flat. If Ty was right, there was only a little time left to solve the mystery and stop Theopolis from ruining Brack's farewell show—and taking the hotel from him. He ran the whole way.

At the Abracadabra, the lobby was totally packed, just like it had been a week before.

Then he realized that many of the magicians were in costume, as if they were going to perform. He spotted Mr. Thursday, who was wearing his finest tuxedo. He was hauling his case of juggling objects.

And there, by the big window along the front wall, were Mr. Madagascar and Dotty. Mr. M. was in fancy robes, ready to put on a show. Dotty was in her old-time magician's assistant outfit: a leotard and high-heel shoes.

Over by the box office, Charlie saw Theopolis. As usual, a group of hangers-on and reporters surrounded him. Among them was Ty.

Charlie hurried over. "What are you doing?" he hissed, tugging on Ty's maroon jacket sleeve.

Ty shushed him. Then he raised his hand and called out, "Mr. Theopolis, sir?"

The crowd hushed. Ty's voice was loud enough to be heard over all the reporters.

"Who said that?" Theopolis said, looking around. "Oh," he said when he spotted Ty. "What do you want?"

"Well, sir," Ty said. Charlie could tell he was doing his best not to smile. "You're all dressed for a show tonight," Ty went on. "But you're not on the marquee outside the hotel. Mr. Abracadabra is."

"If your old friend Brack hasn't figured out the illusion in my performance at his party by now," Theopolis said, "I don't think he will in the next thirty minutes."

"I think I see what you're getting at," Charlie whispered to Ty. Then he said out loud to Theopolis, "Will you share the stage with any other performers?"

"Of course," said Theopolis haughtily. "I

never perform alone. Other magicians are helpful for getting the crowd warmed up."

He smiled hugely and looked out over the faces of reporters nearby. "Of course," he added, "since I'm the greatest magician ever to live, they can't help but pale in comparison to me. They agree to join me because they know I can lift them to greatness."

The press laughed and cheered. Theopolis's assistants clapped and threw flower petals over him.

But not everyone was cheering. Charlie looked for Mr. Madagascar. The levitationist's face was bent in an angry scowl, and his arms were crossed over his chest.

Mr. Thursday was standing there too. He held a bowling pin in one hand and slapped it into his other hand over and over.

"If looks could kill, huh?" Ty said, nodding toward Mr. Thursday.

Charlie sighed.

Dotty Drake was between the two men, with her hands on her hips. She shifted and glared at Theopolis as the press cheered for him. The three of them looked pretty mad.

"We better find Brack," Charlie said. "He only has a few minutes to win this bet."

"And I know how he can do it," Ty added.

* * *

"I had a hunch we'd find you here," Ty called as he and Charlie stepped off the elevator.

Brack stood up from his spot beneath a tree on the Abracadabra Hotel's roof. "How did you two get up here?" he said, but he didn't seem angry.

Ty held up his key ring. "Turns out Rocky had the extra key," he said.

Brack shrugged. "I had to make a copy for emergencies," he said. "Are you here to say good-bye?"

"Of course not," Charlie said. "But we have to hurry and get downstairs before the show starts."

"Right," said Ty. "You've got to get on that stage and announce that you've won the bet."

"I haven't," Brack said sadly. "I'm sorry, boys. I don't know how he did it."

"We do," Ty said.

"We'll explain everything on the way down," said Charlie.

23 Assistance

The theater was packed. Every seat was full, and some people were even standing up behind the back rows, even way up in the balcony.

When Brack stepped into the theater with Charlie and Ty, he practically bumped into Theopolis.

The demonic magician stood in his black robe near the doors, an assistant on each side. He was waiting, it seemed, for the wager deadline to arrive.

"Brack," he said through a toothy grin. "How noble of you to come down to the theater, despite your failure."

Brack put out his hand to shake and Theopolis accepted.

The crowd grew silent. Charlie could feel the people around him straining to hear the conversation between the two great illusionists.

"You are a wise man," Theopolis said. "You have lost with grace. And since you're here, you've saved me the considerable trouble of sending security to remove you from my new rooftop estate."

Brack smiled, and then he continued his walk down the aisle toward the stage. Charlie and Ty hurried after him. "Where do you think you're going?" Theopolis hollered after them.

"You won't be taking that stage tonight, nor ever again!"

Brack did not stop. He took the steps up the stage. Theopolis tried to follow, but Charlie and Ty stepped in front of him, blocking his path.

"Out of my way, children," Theopolis said. "This theater belongs to me. I shall have you thrown out!" He thrust his finger in the air as he spoke.

"It's not yours yet," said Charlie. He checked his watch. "Brack has ten minutes."

Ty smirked. "Why don't you take a seat?" hc said. "I'm sure Brack would be happy to give you his box seat in the front."

"Yeah. He won't need it!" Charlie said.

The boys laughed and Theopolis glowered at them.

A stagehand hurried to push out a lectern. There was some hurried chatter in the wings and in the catwalk, and a spotlight thumped on.

"Ladies and gentlemen," Brack said, "and

children of all ages. I have a couple of announcements."

The crowd went silent.

"First of all, the performance tonight will not go on as scheduled," Brack said.

Theopolis smiled. "A concession speech," he said. He smirked at Charlie and Ty. "Such class."

"It will unfortunately begin a few minutes late," Brack went on. "I haven't dressed yet, as you can see."

"What?" Theopolis snapped.

"And the second announcement," Brack said, "I only have a few minutes to complete. I shall now reveal how Theopolis performed his levitation trick—yes, trick, not magic—at my party last weekend."

Theopolis gasped. "Impossible!" he said. "Get down from that stage at once!"

Ty and Charlie held Theopolis's arms to stop him from rushing the stage.

"I would like some assistance, however,"

Brack said. "I will ask three excellent performers to join me onstage. I think they're here in the theater."

The crowd of magicians began to chatter. It could be any three of them, they hoped.

"Expert juggler, Mr. Thursday," Brack said. Mr. Thursday stood up in the back row and the crowd applauded slightly.

"Mr. Madagascar," Brack said, "a resident of this very hotel. The brilliant levitator and illusionist!"

Mr. Madagascar, who was seated along the wall near the front, stood up and bowed. The crowd applauded, a little louder this time, and he waved.

"And finally," Brack said, "Dotty Drake, one of the finest magician's assistants ever to grace this theater."

Dotty jumped to her feet. She was sitting on the aisle quite close to the stage. The crowd went wild with applause.

The three performers, all dressed in their finest show clothes, climbed the stage and joined Brack at the lectern.

"Theopolis would like us to believe that he is the greatest magician of all time," Brack said. "He'd like us to believe that he can do alone what most of us need help to do."

Theopolis backed away from the stage a little.

"This is a shame," Brack went on, "because Theopolis is a fine illusionist, and a true master of modern magic techniques." Brack smiled and shrugged shyly. "I admit, most of his special effects go right over my old head," he added. The audience chuckled.

"But when he needed help in his schemes," Brack said, his face going serious, "he knew he'd need assistance from these three."

The other three performers on stage took a bow.

"Thursday here was the juggler we all saw

over the pool," Brack explained. "He dressed in a robe just like Theopolis's, and the two switched places."

"It was easy in the crowd and the smoke," Charlie said, glaring at Theopolis.

"Of course," Brack went on, "Thursday wasn't actually over the pool. He was hidden away, with Madagascar and Theopolis."

Madagascar looked at his feet.

"It was Madagascar's mirrors that made Thursday appear to be levitating," Brack said. "And it was Theopolis's projector that made Thursday appear to be over the pool."

"The smoke again," Charlie said. "It was thick and white enough to act as a screen."

"And Dotty," Brack said, "the assistant, simply made sure everything went off without a hitch. She operated the smoke machine, very likely, and aimed the projector."

Dotty nodded.

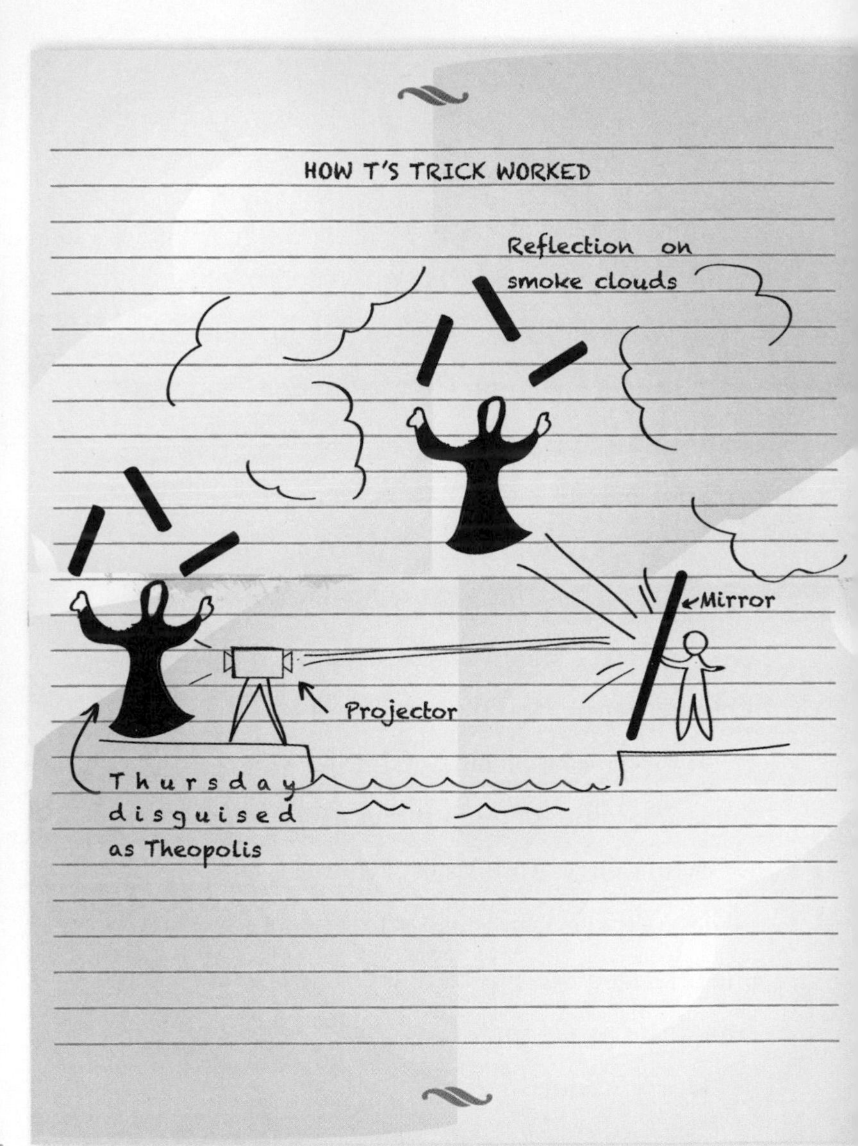
HOW T'S TRICK WORKED
Reflection on smoke clouds
Mirror
Projector
Thursday disguised as Theopolis

When Brack's explanation was complete, the crowd cheered.

"Your applause should be directed toward these four performers," Brack said. "Not me." He waved at Theopolis, calling him onstage. "It was a wonderful illusion," Brack said gently.

Theopolis slowly joined the others in the center of the stage.

"And now, our show can begin," Brack said. "I will go backstage and prepare, and these four will be . . . my opening act."

He winked at Theopolis and disappeared into the wings.

To open, Theopolis and the others performed a repeat of the trick from the party, without the pool.

No one was very impressed this time, but all of the magicians clapped hard to cheer for Mr. Thursday, Mr. Madagascar, and Dotty Drake.

By the time they were done, Brack—now fully Abracadabra—was dressed.

He stepped onto the stage.

The stage lights went black, and the spotlight thumped on again and shined on the greatest magician of all time.

Abracadabra then performed an illusion so great, so brilliant, and so completely unexplainable that the finest minds in the world are still trying to figure out just how he did it.

Of course, Charlie knows.

MICHAEL DAHL grew up reading everything he could find about his hero Harry Houdini, and worked as a magician's assistant when he was a teenager. Even though he cannot disappear, he is very good at escaping things. Dahl has written the popular Library of Doom series, the Dragonblood books, and the Finnegan Zwake series. He currently lives in the Midwest in a haunted house.

LISA K. WEBER is an illustrator currently living in Oakland, California. She graduated from Parsons School of Design in 2000 and then began freelancing. Since then, she has completed many print, animation, and design projects, including graphic novelizations of classic literature, character and background designs for children's cartoons, and textiles for dog clothing.